Mr. Munday and the Rustlers

Designed by Rebecca Tachna. Manufactured in Spain.

10 9 8 7 6 5 4 3 2 1

Library of Congress Cataloging in Publication Data

Pryor, Bonnie. Mr. Munday and the rustlers. Summary: Mr. Munday, a bumbling mailman, outwits ornery rustlers when he and his cat take care of a farm. [1. Robbers and outlaws—Fiction. 2. Farms—Fiction. 3. Cats—Fiction. 4. Postal service—Letter carriers—Fiction]
I. Manyum, Wallop, ill. II. Title. III. Title: Mister Munday and the rustlers.   PZ7.P49465Mp 1987 [E] 87-17539
ISBN 0-13-604737-8

Mr. Munday and the Rustlers

BY BONNIE PRYOR
ILLUSTRATED BY WALLOP MANYUM

PRENTICE HALL BOOKS FOR YOUNG READERS A DIVISION OF SIMON & SCHUSTER INC., NEW YORK

CHAPTER
♦♦♦♦♦♦♦♦♦♦♦
ONE

♦♦♦♦♦

Mr. Munday was a mailman. He lived in a little white house at the end of a winding street. In his front yard was an old apple tree with blossoms in the spring and crunchy sweet apples in the fall. In his backyard was a strawberry patch with berries for making jam or eating with sugar and milk. And in the window of the little white house sat a fat cat named Harry. Harry waited patiently while Mr. Munday was away delivering the mail. When he returned, Harry rubbed against his leg as if to say, *I've missed you. Now hurry up and get my supper.*

Every day when Mr. Munday got up he brushed his teeth exactly twenty times going up and twenty times going down. Then he made breakfast for himself and poured Harry a bowl of milk.

"Fiddlesticks," Mr. Munday said to Harry one night. "I am ever so tired of doing the same thing every day. Tomorrow I am going to have an adventure."

The next morning Mr. Munday got up ten minutes later than usual. He only brushed his teeth ten times each way. He didn't wash his breakfast dishes, and he decided to give Harry his milk at night instead of in the morning. Harry did not like the change at all. He sat in Mr. Munday's favorite chair all day and sulked.

As for Mr. Munday, when he delivered the mail on

Mulberry Street he thought about all the dishes he would have to wash when he got home. On Elm Street and Oak Street and Birch Street, he worried about Harry at home without any milk.

"My stars," said Mr. Munday when he got home. "This is not a good way to have an adventure. I will have to think of something else." He gave Harry an extra big bowl of milk and some tuna for a treat. But Harry was so mad he would not even meow a thank-you.

The next morning Mr. Munday delivered a letter to himself.
It was from Cousin Arthur who lived on a farm not far from
the city. This is what it said.

Dear Mr. Munday,
I must take
a trip to the
city. Please
come and take
care of my animals
especially Betsy,
my Prize-winning
cow.
Cousin Arthur

"By George, I'll do it," said Mr. Munday. "It will be a real
adventure." He ran all the way home and packed his bag.
Then he grabbed Harry, who was not pleased at all, and
headed straight for Cousin Arthur's farm.

◆◆◆

CHAPTER

◆◆◆◆◆◆◆◆◆◆◆

TWO

Cousin Arthur was a tall skinny man who didn't like to work. Every year he invited someone to stay on his farm so he could take a vacation.

"You are just in time," he told Mr. Munday. "Now all you have to do is feed the chickens and milk the cows. Then you can paint the barn and fix the fence—and don't forget to gather the eggs and plow the field."

Before he left, Cousin Arthur showed Mr. Munday his cows. "This is Buttercup and Mabel. And this is Clarabelle and Dumpling. And this is Betsy, my prize-winning cow. Take good

care of her. I would be very unhappy if anything happened to Betsy."

Mr. Munday looked at Clarabelle and Dumpling. He looked at Buttercup and Mabel. Then he looked at Betsy. All of the cows were brown and white. They all had soft brown eyes and a tail to brush away the flies.

"Wait," cried Mr. Munday. "How will I remember which cow is Betsy?" But it was too late. Cousin Arthur had already left.

"My stars," said Mr. Munday. "What shall I do?" Then he had a wonderful idea.

Mr. Munday went to the barn. He found a bucket of red paint and a brush.

"I will paint a nice red spot on Betsy," Mr. Munday said to himself. "Then she will not look like the other cows."

But Betsy did not want to be painted. She kicked over the bucket of red paint and ran to the other side of the pasture.

The red paint splashed all over the ground, and all over Mr. Munday and Harry. Some of it splashed on Betsy's hooves.

"Galloping grasshoppers," wailed Mr. Munday. "I did not know that cows do not like to be painted. Cousin Arthur is not going to be happy to see red paint all over his farm."

Mr. Munday cleaned up the paint. Then he fed the chickens and gathered the eggs. He plowed the field and milked the cows. By evening he was so tired he could hardly move. He went straight to bed.

Harry was not tired. He had slept all day in Cousin Arthur's favorite chair. He squeezed out a window to catch a fat mouse for a late-night snack. But as he crossed the barnyard, he saw a truck parked by the cow pasture and two men sneaking through the bushes.

Big Bad Bob was a rustler. He was big and fat, and he could burp louder than anyone in the world. His partner, Sneaky Pete, was little and mean. He wiped his nose on the back of his hand as they looked over Cousin Arthur's cows.

"This is the best bunch of cows we ever rustled," said Big Bad Bob. "After we sell them, I will be rich."

"You mean we'll be rich, don't you?" whined Sneaky Pete.

"Of course," said Big Bad Bob with an evil grin. "Don't I always share?"

Just then Sneaky Pete took a step backwards and—crunch—he stepped right on Harry's tail. Harry let out a sound that was like a screech and a holler rolled up together. It was as loud as three fire engine sirens and a church bell all going off at the same time.

Sneaky Pete and Big Bad Bob jumped twenty feet in the air. The noise woke Mr. Munday out of his sound sleep. He ran out the door just in time to see the rustlers hightail it back to the truck and take off in a cloud of dust. They didn't even wait to load Clarabelle, Dumpling, Mabel and Buttercup. But Betsy was already on the truck.

◆◆◆

CHAPTER

♦♦♦♦♦♦♦♦♦♦♦

THREE

♦♦♦

Poor Mr. Munday didn't know what to do. He went back
into the house and sat in Cousin Arthur's second favorite
chair. On the wall by the chair was a picture of Cousin Arthur
and Betsy wearing her blue first-prize ribbon. That gave Mr.
Munday an idea. He drew a picture of a cow. It was brown
and white with soft brown eyes and a tail to brush away the
flies. And it had red hooves. When he was done Mr. Munday
went to town to see the sheriff.

"Sounds like Big Bad Bob and Sneaky Pete," said the
sheriff when Mr. Munday had told him about Cousin Arthur's

prize-winning cow. "No one can find their secret hideaway. And even if we did, how could you tell which cow is Betsy? All cows look alike."

"This cow is different," said Mr. Munday. He showed the sheriff the picture of Betsy.

"I saw a chicken with purple feathers once," said the sheriff. "But I never saw a cow with red hooves."

Mr. Munday went back to the farm. He fed the chickens and gathered the eggs. He worried all day, but by nightfall he had thought of a plan.

"Harry," he said. "Those rustlers will be mad that they did not get all the cows. They might even come back tonight. If I looked like a cow, then the rustlers might take me, too."

"Meow," said Harry. He licked his sore tail.

Mr. Munday looked all over Cousin Arthur's house for something that would make him look like a cow. At last he

found a bearskin rug in the parlor. It was furry and brown, and it had sharp teeth.

"This does not look very much like a cow," said Mr. Munday. "But it is the best I can do. Maybe Big Bad Bob will not notice in the dark."

That night Mr. Munday crawled under the bearskin rug and pinned on Betsy's blue ribbon. Then he crept to the pasture.

All the cows were asleep. They did not see the new cow. But someone else was there, and he noticed the new cow.

Sneaky Pete wiped his nose on the back of his hand. "Cousin Arthur has a new cow," he said. "She doesn't look like a cow at all, but she has won a blue ribbon."

"Moo, Mooo," said Mr. Munday in his best cow voice.

"Put her in the truck," said Big Bad Bob. "Cousin Arthur has strange-looking cows. Remember the one with red feet?" Big Bad Bob was thinking about the money he was going to get for all those fancy cows. And he wasn't going to share any of it with Sneaky Pete. Robbers never share.

Sneaky Pete pushed Mr. Munday onto the truck and slammed the doors. The truck bumped down the road to the rustlers' secret hideaway with Clarabelle, Dumpling, Mabel, Buttercup and a furry brown cow with sharp bear teeth.

◆◆◆

CHAPTER

FOUR

The old truck weaved around corners and bounced over rocks. Clarabelle stepped on Mr. Munday's toes three times, and once Mabel almost sat on him before the truck arrived at the hideaway.

"Put these new cows in the pasture," Big Bad Bob said to Sneaky Pete. "I'm going to bed."

"I'm tired too," whined Sneaky Pete. But he knew better than to argue with Big Bad Bob. He opened the door and shooed Clarabelle, Dumpling, Mabel and Buttercup into the pasture. Mr. Munday had to hop on his sore toes. Then the

bearskin rug caught on a rusty nail. Mr. Munday tried to
wiggle back into it, but it was too late. Sneaky Pete was
looking straight at him. "Ah ha!" said Sneaky Pete. "Wait
until I tell Big Bad Bob!"

"Why are you helping Big Bad Bob?" asked Mr. Munday,
thinking fast. "Especially when he is not going to share with
you."

"He promised," said Sneaky Pete.

"I wouldn't believe him if I were you," said Mr. Munday.
"I'll bet he never shares."

Sneaky Pete forgot all about Mr. Munday. He stomped into
the house. "How come you didn't share your candy bar
yesterday?" he shouted. "You never even gave me a bite."

Mr. Munday didn't wait to hear more. He grabbed the bear
suit and ran to town as fast as he could.

◆◆◆

CHAPTER

◆◆◆◆◆◆◆◆◆◆

FIVE

◆◆◆

The rustlers' hideaway was a long way from town. Mr. Munday was still walking the next morning when the sun came up. It was getting warm, and the bear suit was itchy and hot. He was still trudging along when Big Bad Bob and Sneaky Pete passed him with a truck load of cows. They saw Mr. Munday, but they just waved and laughed.

Mr. Munday was feeling pretty bad right about then. Maybe that is why he did what he did. Mr. Munday was a very tidy man. He would never even drop a candy wrapper on the street. But when he dropped the bearskin rug, he didn't even stop to pick it up!

All of a sudden there were red lights flashing and sirens screaming. The sheriff and fourteen deputies surrounded Mr. Munday.

"Litterbug!" shouted the sheriff. "Litterbug!" the deputies yelled. Mr. Munday had never been so ashamed in all his life. On the way back to town, Mr. Munday tried to tell the sheriff about the rustlers. "Hrumpf," said the sheriff. "How could you find the rustlers faster than my fourteen deputies?"

There was no sign of Big Bad Bob and Sneaky Pete
anywhere in town. There was someone selling cows to a crowd
of farmers. But it was a fine English gentleman named Sir
Robert Percival.

"Sir Robert is ever so sad to part with his cows," said Master Peter, his butler. "Why he loves them as if they were his own children."

Sir Robert dabbed at his eyes with a handkerchief and

burped delicately. "How true," he sighed.

Mr. Munday looked at Sir Robert's cows. They were all brown and white. They all had soft brown eyes and a tail to brush away the flies. But one cow was different. One cow had red feet. "That is Betsy," shouted Mr. Munday.

"Nonsense," said Sir Percival. "All cows look alike."

"Not Betsy," said the sheriff. He pulled out the picture of Betsy. "See, she has red feet."

"I think that is my Susie," said a farmer.

"That's my Francine," shouted another farmer.

The sheriff grabbed Sir Robert Percival and Master Peter just as they were tiptoeing away. "I think we had better have a long talk about cows," he said, dragging Big Bad Bob and Sneaky Pete away to jail. "We won't have to worry about these two for a long time," he said. "Thanks to Mr. Munday."

"Hooray," yelled all the farmers. "Hooray for Mr. Munday."

Mr. Munday rounded up all of Cousin Arthur's cows and took them home. Harry was glad to see him. He rubbed against his leg as if to say, *I forgive you, even though you did forget to feed me.* Mr. Munday gave Harry his milk and took Cousin Arthur's cows back to the pasture. Just then Cousin Arthur came back home.

"I suppose being on a farm wasn't every exciting," he said. "But you have done a fine job. Except for one thing. You really didn't have to paint Betsy's hooves. She is beautiful enough just the way she is."

"Meow," said Harry. Mr. Munday just smiled.

♦♦♦